PRESUMED GUILTY

Contemporary Romantic Suspense

MICHELLE GREY

ISBN-13: 978-1722321550
ISBN-10: 1722321555
Copyright 2018 by Lucky 13 Unlimited
All Rights Reserved.

Except for use in a review, the reproduction or utilization of this work, in whole or in part, in any form, is forbidden without the written permission of the author.

This book is a work of fiction. References to real people, events, establishments, organizations, or locations are intended only to provide a sense of authenticity. All other characters, and all incidents and dialogue, are drawn from the author's imagination and are not to be construed as real.

Cover Art and Design by Cover Me Darling
Formatting by Athena Interior Book Design

To my dear friend, Jill. Every day, in every way, you're getting better and better. Love you, sister.

CHAPTER ONE

Blood spattered against Michael Venetti's jacket a second before he absorbed the impact of Ernie Kinsley's body. He whipped out his gun and scanned the rooftops, but saw nothing. Twenty more steps and he would've delivered the older man safely inside the courthouse. Son of a bitch.

Amid the panic of the growing crowd, Michael holstered the Glock and kneeled next to Kinsley's prone form. A uniformed officer ran around the front of the patrol car clutching a towel. He applied it to the gaping hole in Kinsley's chest as Michael once again assessed the area.

Kinsley gripped Michael's arm, his eyes glazed as he struggled to form words. "Tell Grace to take care." He coughed blood. "Protect her."

Moments later, life left his eyes and body. Emergency personnel rushed onto the scene. Michael stood, Kinsley's words searing him with a jolt of regret. He had to know that Michael was the last person Grace Cooper would turn to for anything. Michael owed her an explanation, the truth she didn't want to hear.

He'd given her the space and time she'd demanded from him, but someone just took out her stepfather and that changed everything.

The overcast skies mirrored Grace's mood as she stared at the flag-draped casket. She and Ernie hadn't been close, but he was the only father she'd ever known. He was a decorated war veteran. He was a disgraced money launderer. He was dead.

Susan had understandably begged off. Grace's sister lived in California and was two weeks away from delivering her first child. But their mother, who'd moved out to Susan's once the news broke about her husband's arrest, had refused to make the trip. So Grace stood alone in the crowd of businessmen and veterans until the casket was lowered into the ground.

Tears threatened as she walked to her car, the echoes of the twenty-one gun salute, and the murmurs from the wagging tongues, still ringing in her ears. Six months ago, her life had been picture perfect. How things had unraveled since then.

"Hello, Grace." Michael Venetti slid into step beside her. His deep voice shook her from her thoughts. "I'm sorry about Ernie."

Her heart bumped in her chest. *Jesus, not now.*

She thought she'd gotten enough emotional distance from him to feel nothing, but the sincerity in his tone wrecked her already frayed nerves. Anger bubbled to the surface. Which part was he sorry for? Dating her to get to Ernie? Arresting him? His death?

She swallowed the bitter words like bile. "Thank you."

"Do you have time for coffee? We need to talk."

Grace stumbled at his audacity. This man who'd put an engagement ring on her finger then walked out of her life on the same day still thought they should talk? Michael reached out to steady her, and she recoiled from the zing his touch still evoked. "I'm busy. And there's nothing left to say, Michael. Pretty sure I've made that clear." She breathed a sigh of relief that he didn't follow her to her car. Her hold on her emotions was tenuous at best.

"There's a lot to say when you're ready to listen." His voice carried in the damp air. "And I'm a patient man."

Grace slammed the car door on his words, then jammed the key into the ignition. Would there ever come a time when he didn't affect her? Not if she stayed here. That much was obvious. She loved Chicago and had lived in the area her entire life, but the pressure to flee was mounting. There was only one thing standing in her way, and in sixty days, she'd be free.

With the keys to her new locks tucked in her pocket, Grace cranked her speaker and jammed to her Eighties hairband playlist. Nothing like a little Def Leppard to shake off the heaviness of yesterday's funeral, and get her motivated to clean. In every house she'd rehabbed, some unwritten rule demanded that former occupants let the place go to hell.

She cleared enough space in the formal living room for her air mattress then propped the broom against the broken fireplace mantel. This place might look like a distressed property to the naked eye, but to her, it was her most ambitious project. The one that, when finished, should allow her enough financial cushion to figure out what and where was next.

Grace used her portable air compressor to blow up the mattress. Living here while she renovated would be an experiment she hoped to never repeat, but her options were nil. Her family home had been sold, her childhood memories packed away in storage. She'd already spent weeks on her friend's couch, and she'd given up her apartment lease based on a lie. Not that she wanted to waste a penny of her budget on living space. She'd be here almost every waking moment anyway.

On the floor next to Grace's work stool, her phone lit up. She checked the caller ID, then set it back on the stool. "Not tonight, Sis," she whispered.

The texts she'd sent to Susan after the funeral would have to hold her over. Grace loved her, but every conversation came around to the seismic shift they'd experienced since their stepfather's arrest. Grace didn't see the point in rehashing any of it. Ernie was gone. And the collateral damage of her broken heart was finally beginning to heal, and would continue to, as long as Michael stayed out of her life.

Seeing him yesterday had led to a restless night filled with memories of their time together, and their aborted plans for the future. Even this property was a reminder. They'd found it and drawn up renovation plans together, considered keeping it for themselves.

Grace ordered a pizza to silence her grumbling stomach, then took the half flight of stairs from the living room up to the kitchen. The open floor concept and the expanse of windows along the back of the house had drawn her the first time she'd seen it. She leaned her head against the wooden window frame, imagining the finished product and the happy family who would eventually call this place home.

It wouldn't be *her* happily ever after, but it would be for someone.

The waning sunlight allowed her enough light to study the perfect, manicured landscapes of the houses that circled the lake. Despite her property's decent outward appearance, she was positive everyone in Stonebrooke Estates knew it was a foreclosure, and was anxious for it to be rescued and restored for their property values' sake.

Grace wanted that more than anyone. Because when this chapter of her life was finished, there would be no more reason for Michael to haunt her dreams.

Michael motioned to the chair across from him and waited for Brian Perry, the Federal agent he'd worked with for the last year and a half, to take a seat. Together they'd closed down the money-laundering ring run by Ernie Kinsley and four other high-profile businessmen. After days of answering repeated questions about the events surrounding Kinsley's murder, Michael was ready to ask his own questions.

"Thanks for swinging by the station," Michael said.

Brian declined the coffee Michael offered with a shake of his head. "No problem. I'd have come by sooner but I was in D.C. Been a hell of a week, huh?"

"That's for damn sure." Michael paused. "What's this do to our case?"

Tossing his glasses on the desk, Brian squeezed the bridge of his nose. "It'll go on. We're airtight. We'll still get convictions."

Puzzled by his dark tone, Michael crossed his arms. "You make that sound like a bad thing. We shut down one of the biggest money laundering operations since Wachovia."

"Pale in comparison." Brian met Michael's frown. "Kinsley cut a deal with us."

That was one thing Michael liked about Brian. He never had to wait for the punchline. As part of the city team that had coordinated with the FBI, Michael wouldn't have been involved in the negotiations, but the news still caught him by surprise. "What deal?"

Seconds ticked by before Brian spoke. "He gave us names, Michael. Big names. Powerful names. A U.S. Senator among them. Hinted at extortion, even murders for hire. We kept it as quiet as possible, but someone who knew about it took him out. We have some details, but no hard proof. Kinsley was supposed to provide that after his court appearance."

Michael contained his frustration, but damn. That might've been good information to know before he marched Kinsley toward the courthouse and his death. "Now what?"

Brian threw up his hands. "Now we start over. Try to build the case without him."

Michael felt the squeeze of uncertainty in his chest as Ernie's last words rang in his ears. Elbows on the table, he leaned in. He respected Brian, but still thought twice before he spoke. "You think there's another way to get the proof he had."

Brian's shrewd eyes narrowed. "Is that a statement or a question?"

"Both." Michael didn't flinch. "I need to know why Kinsley's last words were a warning to protect his stepdaughter, and whether it has anything to do with your deal."

Silence filled the small room, and Michael got the distinct impression he was being weighed on an invisible scale. Metal chair legs scraped along the tile floor as Brian stood, his hard look daunting.

"Kinsley said he had insurance. A data backup. We confiscated his corporate and personal computers and didn't find shit. We're keeping this possibility buttoned up as tight as we can."

Just like they thought they kept the deal quiet. Uneasiness shifted to urgency. He couldn't assume Grace was safe. She might not want to see him, but he *had* to see her, talk to her.

"You could help us out here, Michael. I know you don't have skin in this game, but we need to know what Grace Cooper knows ASAP. One of my agents saw you talking to her at the funeral yesterday."

Michael rose, studying the man across from him. He had every intention of seeing Grace again, but he wouldn't do it under false pretenses. "I'll track her down because she needs to know what's going on. If she has information she's willing to give me, I'll let you know."

Brian shook Michael's hand, his grip firm. "You have twenty-four hours, then I'm bringing her in."

His tone made it clear he was issuing a professional courtesy. Nodding, Michael subdued a spark of anger. "Understood."

Mind whirling, Michael returned to his desk. If Brian's case had any legs, he'd do what he could to help, but gaining intel was secondary to protecting Grace. He shoved his laptop into its bag then tugged his jacket from the back of his chair.

"What was Perry doing here?" Jason Nunez, his long-time partner, sat at the desk across from him, popping his bubble gum like a teenager. It used to drive Michael crazy, but it was better than the incessant leg tap that would begin the second the gum went in the trash can. "Haven't seen him around much."

Michael swallowed his growing anxiety as he checked his watch. He had to figure out where to find Grace. "He's been in DC. Just got back and wanted to follow up on Kinsley."

Jason nodded. "Yeah, shitty deal." He stood and stretched. "I'm headed out to play some Texas Hold 'Em. Wanna come so I can clean out your wallet?"

Michael laughed and shook his head. "No time today. And I like hanging on to my money."

He hadn't invested much energy in his social calendar. Hadn't even seen his cabin in Door County all season. Nothing felt right without Grace by his side, but that didn't keep Jason from trying to fill up his evenings.

Jason blew a bubble then popped it. "Your loss. I won three hundred bucks last week."

"That should help make up for the five hundred you lost the week before."

Michael dodged the pencil Jason threw at him as dispatch came over the radio requesting a response to a noise complaint at 318 Sandy Avenue. It only took a second for the address to click in Michael's brain, sending a quick, hard punch straight to his chest. That address, plus a noise complaint, could only mean one thing. Grace had closed on their property.

Her property, he corrected.

Relief flooded through him at his good fortune. "Hey," he hollered to Jason as he strode to the door. "Tell dispatch not to send a patrolman. I'll run over there myself and take a look."

Jason jumped up from his desk, wearing a frown. "You'd rather spend your evening checking out a noise complaint?"

"It's Grace's new rehab. I need to catch up with her."

"Damn, dude." Jason shook his head. "Why keep letting her break your heart? She ain't worth it."

Michael held his tongue, and his temper. He tried to keep his personal life private, but Jason was too close, knew too much. *Or at least he thought he did.* He had no idea Michael had proposed to Grace. And he damn sure hadn't heard the tears in Grace's voice when Michael shocked her by walking away.

A hard knock at the front door jarred Grace from her thoughts. Had to be a new record for the pizza guy. Nice selling point for the house, maybe. After turning down the music, she dug bills out of her purse then opened the door. Her breath caught in her throat as Michael stood there, blue eyes shadowed in the bright porch light.

She tamped down the unwanted twinge of attraction, and her surprise at seeing him two days in a row, and tried for a neutral tone. "What are you doing here?"

"Got a noise complaint at the station."

Bristling, she crossed her arms. "From who?"

Michael tilted his head slightly to the right and pulled out a citation book.

Her eyes widened. "You've got to be kidding me. You're going to write me a ticket?"

He gave her a sideways grin that took her all the way back to the first night she met him at a friend's party. "Pretty unhappy neighbor." He shrugged. "You going to let me in?"

The urge to turn him away simmered in her chest. She was on a better emotional plane than yesterday, but overall, her pride was still more than a little wounded. There was no way she wanted to pay for a freaking ticket, though. Or let him know the effect he still had on her. She opened the door just wide enough for him to walk through. If she played nice, maybe he would, too.

He glanced around the interior. "Doesn't look any different than it did a few months ago. Still a hell of a lot of potential."

"Give me time. I just got the keys today."

"Which explains why we got our first noise complaint tonight."

At one time, she would've appreciated the humor in his tone. Instead, she shrugged it off. "I'll try to keep it down."

The doorbell rang again, and Grace pulled the money back out of her pocket. She thanked the delivery driver, barely suppressing a groan of appreciation as the scent of pepperoni and yeasty crust wafted around her. She headed to the kitchen and slid the pizza box onto a small section of remaining counter top.

Michael was close behind her when she turned, his voice low. "I wasn't criticizing your progress, just observing. And remembering."

His nearness almost overwhelmed her good sense. She closed her eyes for a brief moment against the powerful temptation to lean into him, to feel his arms come her. Her brain argued that she should tell him to leave. Take the damn ticket to preserve her sanity.

Fool that she was, she ignored the wisdom and offered him a paper plate instead. "I'm starving." She pulled a steaming piece of pizza from the box then stepped away to get some distance from Michael. "Help yourself if you're hungry. I don't have a refrigerator for leftovers."

He didn't comment on her quick getaway. Instead, he walked around the room as he ate, studying the space, and Grace could almost guarantee he was taking mental notes. Mental notes that she valued, despite the circumstances. The son of a trade carpenter, Michael had had a great eye for the other three properties he'd helped her flip. She swallowed a cheesy bite, and her pride, then walked over to him. "What do you see?"

By the time they'd toured the upstairs and the main floor, she had two pages of notes. So many things she'd forgotten. With a few of his suggestions, she might even be able to trim her budget by a couple thousand.

"Thanks for the insights," Grace said as Michael followed her back to the kitchen. She ripped open a case of water and tossed a bottle to him. "I'm sure you probably need to get going."

More like she needed him to get going. The last thirty minutes proved it would be all too easy to let her guard down.

"You'd mentioned the patio and outdoor space. Let's see what kind of ideas we come up with out there."

17

Self-preservation mode kicked in and Grace folded her arms. "It's dark."

He opened the sliding glass door and looked up. There's a fixture. Got any lightbulbs?" She paused, but he pressed on. "Fifteen minutes. Tops."

She shook her head, but went and found one of her packs of bulbs. "Fifteen minutes," she echoed, handing one to him.

He screwed in the bulb, which didn't do much for the yard, but cast the patio in soft light. Too soft. Too romantic. God, he was bad for her peace of mind.

She swallowed hard. "On second thought, maybe this wasn't a good idea."

"Grace."

Her name, soft on his lips, drew her up short. Their gazes locked, memories and broken trust surfacing all over again. She held up her hands as he walked toward her, the hard shake of her head sending her ponytail dancing on her shoulders. "We're not going there."

Michael opened his mouth to respond as a sharp series of barks erupted from behind the neighbor's fence.

With a silent sigh of relief, Grace stepped back. Part of her had wanted to hear what he would say next. The insane, glutton-for-punishment part. She schooled her features, anxious to get off the roller coaster and back on solid ground.

She jerked her head toward the neighbor's privacy fence. "Before you go, maybe you can issue a ticket for her yapping dog," she joked.

Michael's face turned flinty. "Listen, Grace. I didn't come here to issue a noise citation. I came here because you may be in danger."

CHAPTER TWO

The conflict in Grace's body language, and in her deep brown eyes, since she'd let him in the house gave Michael a spark of hope. He wanted nothing more than to explain why he'd walked away from her, and how much he's hated every day since then.

By the skepticism screaming from her arched brow though, his window of opportunity was closing to say what had to be discussed first. And there was no way he was leaving without doing a perimeter scan.

"Walk with me?" He nodded toward the far corner of the house, relieved when after a pause, she fell into step beside him. "You know I was with Ernie before he died." She gave a short nod. "His final words were very clear. He told me to protect you."

"What?" Grace crossed her arms as if warding off a chill, her brow furrowed in the waning light. "That doesn't make any sense. I haven't even talked to him since his arrest. Why would he say that?"

Michael had considered on the drive over how to answer that question, but there was nothing he could say to sugarcoat the truth, nor did he want to. Somehow, he had to thread the needle between convincing her this was serious and scaring the crap out of her.

"He cut a deal with the Feds to turn over information to bring down some high-ranking people."

"Like who?"

"I don't know. I don't have names."

"You don't know. Or you won't say." The shutters came down over her eyes, and her voice got colder. "Like I said, whatever Ernie had going on had nothing to do with me. He and I rarely spoke, and certainly not about anything important."

"Whoever killed Ernie knew about the deal, Grace. They don't know you weren't close to him. We have to assume there's a threat."

They rounded the corner to the front of the house. A breeze came up, as cool as the look on Grace's face as she climbed the porch steps. Her hand rested on the door handle as she turned to face him. "I appreciate your concern, but there is no 'we,' Michael.

And, like I said, I have nothing to do with anything Ernie was involved in."

He stepped toward her, and ran a hand through his hair. "You still have my number?"

The question was uncomfortable, but important.

She shrugged. "I'm sure."

Michael released the breath he held. "Call me if anything comes to mind. A conversation. A reference. Anything."

The door opened and she stepped over the threshold then turned toward him, squaring her shoulders. "Goodbye, Michael."

The lights from inside the house cast her face in shadow, but the doubt lingering in her dark eyes skewered him. "Goodnight, Grace."

The quiet click as Grace closed the door echoed in the silence Michael left behind. She blew out a breath, daunted by how much energy he took with him. To offset the tangible loss, she grabbed her gloves and broom then attacked the kitchen floor with a vengeance. It was bad enough that Michael's presence disrupted her so easily, but his comments about Ernie had sent a ripple of unease through her.

Like most kids with their parents, she'd paid little attention to Ernie's work. He was gone most of the time anyway, which she assumed was the trade-off for the fact that they had plenty of money. When she decided to quit college to flip houses, he'd been mildly surprised, but not discouraging. He'd even seeded her the money for her first house, which she paid him back with interest. Her throat tightened as she remembered the pride in his eyes the day she wrote that check.

She swallowed hard, and swept harder. Grief was weird.

By the time she was finished, the main floor was as clean as she could get it, and she was exhausted, physically and mentally. She turned off the lights, then pulled the hair tie from her ponytail and massaged her scalp. The air mattress was hard as a rock, but it felt good to stretch her tired muscles. It had been a while since she'd been on this side of the rehab process.

As the quiet house settled, memories of late night demolition, and shared beers and laughter with Michael, bombarded her. Such good times. Times she thought would never end. She wasn't so naïve anymore, but God, why did he still have the power to muddle her mind?

Conflicting, drifting thoughts were slowly disrupted by the neighbor's barking dog. She groaned, wondering how that little twerp might affect her resale value.

Grace rolled on to her side and pulled her pillow over her head. Sleep was essential to her plan. But if anything, the dog's barking only increased. Finally, she sat up, ready to march to the neighbor's house to get them to shut up the dog.

The hair on the back of her neck rose as a scratching noise at the back of the house drew her attention. The barking became even more insistent, and somewhere in Grace's foggy brain, it suddenly seemed like a warning. Michael's words pounded her. *You may be in danger. Danger. Danger.* She fought the air bed then grabbed her phone from the floor next to her. With shaking fingers, she pulled up Michael's number. Pride be damned.

He picked up the call on the first ring and before she spoke, his urgent whisper filled her ear. "I'm at the front door, Grace. Open it."

"My door? How?"

"I never left. I was down the street."

She scurried toward the door and flipped the deadbolt, ignoring the ping of relief that he hadn't left her. "I think —" Glass shattered somewhere in the back of the house, freezing her train of thought.

"Stay here," he commanded.

Fear slithered up her spine as Michael pulled a gun from his waistband and moved toward the stairs to the basement. Fear for herself. Fear for Michael.

Grace strained to hear over the roar of her pounding heartbeat. Scenarios she didn't want to consider skittered at the edge of her brain, but she pushed them away. Instead, she concentrated on her breathing, willing herself to be still.

What felt like an hour later, the stairs creaked, and she realized the dog had stopped barking. Whispered words that she hoped formed some kind of cohesive prayer fell from her lips as the distinct outline of Michael's broad shoulders came into view. She launched into his arms, dizzying relief flowing through her veins.

His arm snaked around her waist, holding her tightly to him, but his back was rigid. "Son of a bitch must've heard me coming. He broke out the window pane and got the door open, but he was already out the door and racing toward the back of the yard when I got down there. There's not near enough fucking light in that yard."

Grace stepped back from his embrace and studied the taut lines of his face, the urge to soothe him overwhelming. Against her better judgment, she placed a hand on his cheek, the roughness of the day's beard growth teasing her fingers. "I'll replace that door with a steel one. It'll be okay. Chances are it was some vandal who thought this house was still empty. Remember when that happened at the Ash Street property? We came in that day and some kid had a field day with red spray paint."

She'd barely made a dent in the savage anger shooting from his eyes, but his breathing had slowed and she could tell her was hearing her.

"You can't stay here tonight."

A pit formed in Grace's stomach. The idea of staying here alone tonight spooked her, but her options were limited.

Michael put his hands on her shoulders. "It's almost midnight. Come to my place."

Grace rebelled against the thought, dropping her hand. In her current state of mind, the last thing she needed was to spend the night anywhere near Michael.

"If you stay here, I'm staying with you and that tiny air mattress is a joke. There's zero point in wasting money for a few hours in a hotel. You can have my bed. I'll take the couch."

His tone said he was ready and willing to take her on if she was inclined to argue. She closed her eyes against the dull throb starting at the base of her skull as her mind searched for another solution. Michael's suggestion was the most logical one. And she really didn't have the extra cash for a hotel room.

Her limited choices irked her as much as his glare. "Fine. But I'll take the couch."

The smell was the same.

That was the first thing Grace noticed when she walked into Michael's condo. Leather and hints of his cologne. The urge to breathe deeply hit her like a freight train. What the hell was she doing here?

She'd vowed to never speak to him again, and in the span of one evening, she was planning to spend the night at his place. Anger and old resentments teetered close to the surface. What was his end game? She slowed her breathing and rubbed a hand along the back of her neck. Now wasn't the time for a migraine to kick in, but they'd forecasted a storm front coming through and she was running on about four hours of sleep. Maybe a warm shower would take the edge off.

"Can I get you a beer?"

She shook her head at the offer, and the absurdity of the situation.

"Thanks, but no. What I really need is a quick shower and a pillow."

"Of course." He shoved his hands in his pockets. "Bathroom's —"

"Through there. I remember." She took a deep breath, trying to keep the edge of bitterness out of her tone. "Look, Michael. There's no need for this to be awkward. I appreciate you letting me crash here. I'll be out of your hair in the morning."

He started to say something then shook his head. "It's late. We can talk about it tomorrow."

She stalked to the shower and pulled a towel from the linen closet. Words weren't getting past the frustration building in her chest, which was just fine since there was no point in starting an argument that couldn't be finished tonight. Michael was damn good at plucking her strings, and she didn't have the mental energy to play the game.

Grace awoke with blinding pressure pounding her left temple. Fighting against the migraine, she squinted an eye open, not surprised to see the rain pouring down in sheets outside the living room window. Michael's window. She groaned and rolled over, hoping against hope that the last few days were nothing but a bad dream.

Sometime later, she woke again. The clouds were still around, but the rain had stopped. She mustered enough energy to sit up and dig through her purse for her migraine medicine. With a sip from the beer Michael had left for her after her shower, she washed down the pills. Gross, but better than trying to swallow them dry. She relaxed against the couch until the pain in her skull ratcheted down to somewhere close to bearable.

When she was able to open her eyes without the stabbing pain, a note on the coffee table in Michael's bold scrawl drew her attention. He'd gone out to grab her favorite Caramel Snickerdoodle Macchiato. She stared at the note, and her eyes welled with stupid, unexpected tears. How many times had he done that in the past on a lazy Sunday morning?

Today was Sunday, but it wasn't a lazy day. She had to order a new door, connect with her contractors, and revamp some of her plans based on Michael's comments. Above all else, she needed to get out of his home. If last night proved anything, it was that Michael was a drug to her. Within hours, she'd let down her guard. Hell, she'd run into the protection of his arms. Difference was, now she knew what detox felt like, and it wasn't worth it.

She disconnected her phone from the charger and jumped when it rang in her hand. Her sister's number popped up on the screen. With a sigh, she answered.

"Hey, Susan. Sorry I didn't call you back last night."

"Liar. You knew I was just looking for a place to vent."

Grace squeezed her eyes closed. Her sister was nothing if not honest. "Still pretty awful?"

"Other than Mom's chronic complaints about how small our house is, or that we don't have the right food in the pantry, we're doing okay. I keep thinking she's going to wake up some morning and appreciate us. It may not be as nice as she's used to, but it's clean and in a decent area." She sighed. "Ethan gives me the eye at least three times a day. I know he's tired of her being here, but he's too sweet to say anything. Still, this can't be a long-term solution."

Grace was close to elevating them both to sainthood. "Now that Ernie's passed, the assets that were frozen should be accessible to her, right?"

"I have no idea. She'll have to get with her attorney and figure that out. Soon."

The whine level was reaching Grace's threshold. Time to switch gears. "Hopefully she'll be tons of help when the baby comes, right?"

"I hope so," Susan sighed. "That was her logic when she moved here."

"I think it's better for everyone that she's in Cali."

Susan paused. "What's that mean?"

Grace considered keeping Michael and his theories out of the conversation, but it would be even worse if her sister found out later. She went through last night's events as she gathered up her things, massaging her sister's worries until they were manageable.

"Do you think he could be right?"

Grace considered Susan's worry-filled question. "I don't. Ernie never even so much as hinted anything to me. Last night was scary, but in the bright light of day, it's more than likely the break-in was just a vandal or a vagrant."

"You should've never dropped out of college," Susan cried. "Volunteering for Habitat for Humanity was supposed to add to your resumé, not turn you on to house flipping. All I can say is thank God Michael was there."

Grace glanced once more around Michael's place, and considered how different the experience would've been without his strength and calmness. She had to agree with her sister on that point, but she wouldn't put voice to it.

"I better run. I need to get out of here and get to work."

Susan clucked her tongue. "Why? Relax and hang out at Michael's today."

Her sister wasn't stupid, but Grace wished she could reach through the phone and shake her. "I'm going to ignore that."

"Why? Afraid of what might happen?"

Grace opened her mouth to respond then snapped it closed, refusing the bait. She blew out a calming breath. "You sound like a four-year-old. Why? Why? You, my dear sister, seem to have a selective memory."

"I don't think so. I remember that, whatever else Ernie was, he was also a criminal. I remember that Michael's job as a detective intersected with his love life and he had to make a choice." She sighed. "Look, baby girl. I know the way it went down was shitty, but you really need to ask yourself what other choice he had."

Grace closed her eyes, the hurt once again bubbling to the surface. "He used me, Susan."

Her sigh was louder this time. "Think what you want. But I don't believe he knew who you were when you started dating."

"So, at what point did he figure it out?"

"Maybe you should ask him that. He had no reason to propose to you if all he was doing was looking for information."

The words rang through the phone, blasting Grace with their quiet insistence. "Look, I gotta go. Good luck with Mom."

"Yeah, I'm gonna need it. Good luck with Michael."

Her sister disconnected the call, and Grace shook her head. Susan had been on the receiving end of countless, swooning phone calls about the incredible Michael Venetti. She'd also listened through Grace's attempts to salvage a broken heart. She was entitled to her opinion, but Grace knew better than to listen to it.

She locked the condo door behind her then tossed her purse onto the passenger seat and started her car. With two fingers, she pressed against her temples to relieve pressure, and hid behind her sunglasses. The medicine had done its job to a point, but the sky had lightened and she knew better than to give her headache any chance to rear its ugly head again.

Grace pulled into her driveway and glanced down the street where a couple of kids on roller skates zoomed along the sidewalk. She shoved her key in the front door and took two steps into the living room before coming to a dead stop.

Every box and tote she owned was busted open, her belongings strewn around the room. The air mattress was sliced through, and her speaker smashed on the floor. She stifled her gasp, afraid of the possibility that whoever did this was still in her house.

As quietly as she could, she closed and locked the door then ran back to her car. She was two blocks away and out of the neighborhood before her heart rate settled down. With a deep, calming breath, she tried to think clearly as she rolled to a stop at a red light. Did this lend credence to her theory, or Michael's?

The only thing to do was go back to his place. She'd have to file a police report either way, and it would be easier to not have to explain the entire situation, especially since the dull throb in her head had returned.

She made the left turn, her gaze flashing to her rear view mirror as tires squealed on a blue sedan screaming through the intersection behind her. She switched to the right lane to get out of the way, but the car slowed and tucked in behind her. Frowning, she did her best to ignore the tailgater. Half a block later, she switched lanes again, and they moved with her.

With one eye on her mirror and the other watching the road, Grace fished through her purse and found her phone. After dialing Michael's number, she picked up speed and slotted into the right lane. On a whim, she made a quick right turn, her head pounding even more as the car braked hard and continued to follow her. Adrenaline spiked through her.

"Come on, Michael," she whispered. "Pick up the phone."

CHAPTER THREE

Michael hurried up the sidewalk, doughnut bag between his teeth, balancing the Starbucks cup holder in one hand and his keys in the other. He wasn't above exploiting Grace's love of coffee and chocolate frosted doughnuts with sprinkles to get her to stay long enough to hear him out. Should've pushed through and forced a conversation last night, but he knew she'd reached her limit.

His message, tweaked between morning stops, was ready. The moment he'd waited for was finally here. The key twisted in the lock, and he pushed open the door, careful to step in quietly in case she was still sleeping. In the dim light, the first thing he noticed was her note sitting next to his on the coffee table.

Thank you for everything. Time for me to get back to work.

The doughnuts landed on the table with a thud. What an idiot he was to think she'd stay. He set the coffee down then retraced his steps to the car, as worry flickered to life in his chest. A block down the road, his phone rang in his pocket. Relief trumped his worry as Grace's caller ID lit up his screen.

"You're going to think I'm crazy."

The shakiness in her voice put him instantly on high alert. "Try me."

"I – someone's following me. Aggressively. Like your average road rager times ten. And I know I didn't do anything to piss them off."

During her hurried explanation, his stomach plummeted. She wasn't crazy, and shit just got a lot more real. "Where are you?"

"North Fairway." A pause. "Almost to Townline."

"Okay. Listen. Once you get to Townline, there's a precinct office three blocks east of you. I'm staying on the line, but set the phone in a cup holder and do not stop until you get there. I'll be there in ten minutes."

Noises filled his ear that made him believe she'd followed his instructions, but the resulting silence grated on him as he sped toward her. When he thought she should be there, he started calling her name through the phone, but there was no reply.

Michael raced into the station parking lot and spied Grace's SUV. He slid his car into the spot next to it, and rapped on her window. His pent-up worry overshadowed the relief of seeing her. "Jesus, Grace. Why didn't you answer me, and why the hell didn't you go in?"

She wobbled a bit as she got out of the car, raising a hand to shield her eyes behind her sunglasses. "The car went on by and –"

"Did you get a license plate? Make or model?"

"It was blue. Four doors." She rubbed her temple, a frown puckering her brow. "They tore up my house."

"What? How?"

"Dumped my stuff," She whispered. "Everything shredded."

"Hey."

Grace looked at him, her eyes glassy and unfocused through her shades, and realization dawned.

"Ah, damn. Migraine?"

She started to turn away, but he caught her arm. And there they were – the telltale pinched lines in her face. "Come on. You need rest." She looked like she wanted to put up a fight, but she let him tuck her into his passenger seat. "I probably still have some of your medicine –"

Her eyes were closed, but she stiffened. "I took something this morning."

"I can tell."

His sarcasm went right past her, and the fact that she didn't answer him worried him as much as the paleness of her skin. As gently as he could, he pulled out of the station, anxious to get her home.

Was it odd that he missed this, too? Block by block, memories assailed him. Every part of Grace had stolen his heart the first night he met her. And the following weeks and months convinced him that he was the luckiest man on the planet. They loved the same music, complemented each other's strengths on the rehabs they'd done together, both saw the vision for their future together.

Then he'd proposed and she'd said yes. And he was invincible. Never in a million years could he have envisioned how quickly their world would fall apart.

In the seat next to him, Grace curled into a ball and moaned.

He rubbed a hand along her shoulder and back. He knew that sound. "You need me to stop?"

A slight shake of her head kept him moving forward. When they reached his condo, she leaned on him, moving toward the sofa, but he guided her instead toward his room, whispering what he hoped were the magic words.

"Blackout curtains."

She complied without argument and Michael quickly yanked down the covers. As soon as she lay down, he removed her shoes and helped her tuck a pillow between her knees as she rolled onto her side.

He made a quick trip to the bathroom. "Here. Take this. It's a couple of Tylenol and an Excedrin migraine. Maybe together, they'll help."

She lifted her head enough to sip the water and swallow the medicine, her pain-filled gaze meeting his. "I didn't want to come back here."

Michael brushed back her tousled hair and kissed her on the forehead, his words a whisper. "I didn't want to let you go."

Her eyes slid closed, and he stood, running a hand over his chin as he watched her body slowly relax with the help of the medicine. He softly closed the bedroom door behind him and dialed Brian's number. No more need to speculate. Whoever Ernie had planned to rat out believed that Grace could have the power to nail them.

As soon as Brian picked up the phone, Michael launched. "They're after Grace. They know."

To Brian's credit, he caught on quick. "Son of a bitch. Get her in. I want to question her."

Every protective fiber in Michael's body came to attention, crawling over his skin in a march of abject protest. No way in hell was he complying with that. Brian couldn't protect Grace any more than he'd protected Ernie.

Michael kept the truth as simple as he could. "She went down with a migraine. She'll be out until tomorrow. I've got her. I'll keep her safe."

"Tomorrow then. I need to know what she knows. What has she given you?"

Michael recognized the tone, and the intense urgency behind it. Brian was invested. He wanted this win. If it was as big as he seemed to think, it would push him straight up the ladder. And Michael wondered if Brian wasn't prioritizing that over Grace's safety.

He didn't hedge his answer, though. "Not a damn thing. Until she was almost run down by the goon squad, she believed I was full of shit."

Brian blew out a breath. "Find out the truth, Michael. Either we find it. Or they do."

Grace arched her back and stretched like a cat, more rested than she'd been in days. She burrowed into the pillow, drifting, then reached across the bed for Michael. But her hand landed on cold sheets.

One eye open, she confirmed the empty bed and her brain tried to remember if he had plans today. Of the two of them, he'd always been the early riser. As she came fully awake, she sat upright, recent events erasing her mind fog, and her temporary peace. In its place, a wedge of sadness, and a little bit of fear.

She dangled her legs over the edge of the bed and rolled her neck, relieved that her brain didn't protest. Her sleep had been dreamless, but a glance at the clock and a peek beyond the curtains at the dusky evening sky confirmed that she'd wasted the entire day. Not that she had a clue what to do at this point. Michael's theory obviously had merit.

Thoughts of Michael, and the way he took care of her today, brought her up short. She closed her eyes against the sharp stab in her chest. Now wasn't the time to think about it. About him. Maybe that time would come, but it would have to wait until she could get mental and physical distance.

Shoving away from the window, she slipped on her shoes and walked into the living room. What she needed now was full disclosure about Ernie and the case, and there was only one way to get it.

"Hey," she said softly.

Michael's head whipped around from the computer screen he was studying, a small smile curving his lips. "Headache's gone?"

It was a question, but it wasn't. He'd had enough experience with her migraines, the look on his face confirmed that he already had his answer, but she nodded anyway.

He rose from his chair, and motioned toward the sofa. "Let's have a seat in here. More comfortable."

For him, maybe. Any grogginess from the medicine was gone, leaving her body and mind one hundred percent aware that, as he sat down next to her, his leg was less than four inches from hers. And that the broad expanse of his chest, covered in a black cotton tee, was the center of her vision. Exactly what she didn't need. If anything, he'd become even more toned in the months since they'd been together. And how was that fair?

She checked her meandering thoughts and crossed her arms. *Focus, Grace.* "So, while I was out of it, did you happen to find out who was trying to play grown-up bumper cars with me?"

Michael scowled. "Not funny. I talked to Brian Perry, the lead FBI agent, and he wants me to bring you in. Thinks you'll tell him things you aren't telling me."

Traces of doubt lingered in his words and his gaze, giving her a weapon to strike him with, yet she found herself unwilling to pick it up. "I would tell you if I knew anything."

Had she not been looking at him closely, she'd have missed the slight relaxing of his jaw.

"We need to find whatever it is they think you have. Yesterday. This thing's not going away until we do."

"I know." She nodded then leaned her head against the sofa cushion and weighed her next words. Once upon a time, she'd trusted him without question. Now, she was in the unenviable position of having to give him her trust again. But there were no red flags, no warning bells going off in her brain. "Except for the tools and things I have at the house, everything I own is in a storage unit in Mundelein. I can't even imagine what we're looking for, but if you all think I have it, that's where it would have to be."

Michael glanced at his watch then took her cold hands in his. "We can go tonight, or in the morning. Your call."

The touch of his long fingers was a temptation she didn't need. The sooner she found whatever it was Michael was looking for, the sooner he'd been gone from her life, and she could start over on her quest to forget about him.

She pulled her hands from his and stood. "Let's go."

***

"You hungry?" Michael glanced at Grace's profile as the strobe of the passing street lights reflected the tight lines around her mouth.

She shook her head. "No."

Other than directions to the self-storage lot, she'd retreated into herself. He wished he could read her thoughts. She'd had a scare today, but he couldn't help thinking that in her head, he was still the worst of the bad guys.

Half-past nine, he pulled into the facility and punched in the code she provided. He drove past building after building of orange roll-up doors until she told him to stop. Her keyring jangled as she hopped out of the car and worked the padlock loose.

Michael stepped in front of her and pulled the door up, the metal scraping loudly in the quiet evening. As she flipped on the light, it looked to him like every other storage unit. Boxes and totes. A set of kitchen chairs and table. And the love seat.

Their favorite piece of furniture outside the bedroom. Its legend had been an inside joke between them, a code word out in public. When they'd decided to move in together, he'd insisted that she save it, and swore he'd make room for it at his place. Did it mean anything that she kept it?

"Well, here we are. Where do we start?" The set of her jaw made him wonder if she was wandering down the same memory lane. If so, she obviously wanted to make a U-turn.

He dusted off his hands and checked his impulse to push the issue. "What would Ernie have had access to?"

Grace scanned the small space, nodding toward a half-dozen boxes in the back. "Stuff from their house, I guess. He was never in my apartment."

They moved boxes and made a haphazard walkway toward the rear of the unit. She used her key to cut the tape on one of the boxes, and began rummaging through the papers. Michael gave her space so she had no reason to resent him going through her personal things.

Twenty minutes later, she threw up her hands.

"I have no idea what we're doing here. This is pointless. There's nothing here but my junk."

"Mind if I have a turn?"

She waved her arm toward the stack of boxes then plunked down onto one of the kitchen chairs. "Be my guest."

Michael pulled a box and brought it to the table, another wave of nostalgia hitting him as he glanced through some of the framed pictures from her childhood. They'd discussed kids, and he'd always hoped they'd have girls with the same dark hair and dark eyes as the little cheerleader smiling for the camera. Bitter sadness hit him broadside and his hands stilled.

Grace was out of her chair and beside him in an instant. "What? Did you find something?"

All logic and thought about the right words, the best way, flew out the window. The truth couldn't wait any longer. He set the picture down, and grasped both her hands in his. "I didn't know about Ernie, Grace. I swear to you." Eyes wide, she tried to pull away, but he wasn't letting go. He had to say it all. Now. "I was so in love with you. I still am. And I meant every word I said to you when I proposed."

She was silent for a long minute as he held her gaze. Her nostrils flared and her chin quivered as her eyes filled with tears. "Please don't. I can't do this."

"Give me one chance to say this." Desperation marked his words as he tugged her closer. "I had no idea who he was to you. Hell, I barely knew his name. I was working another angle of the investigation. But that night I walked into your home and you introduced us, I died inside. Because I knew I couldn't jeopardize the investigation by continuing to see you. Couldn't jeopardize your safety, either. There was no choice."

Grace closed her eyes against the naked pain in Michael's voice, and against the rightness of being held in his arms again. He'd walked away from her without a backward glance. How could he expect her to blindly accept his truth now?

She stepped out of his grip, hating the tears that threatened as daggers of old pain and bitterness shot through her. "Even if that's true, you didn't trust me, Michael." She hated the wobble in her voice. "What do you think I'd have done? Run to Ernie and spilled the beans?"

He winced against her words, but stood firm. "You knew what I did for a living. How often did we ever talk about any active investigation?"

She nodded. "Thank you for proving my point."

"*My* point is that it wasn't an issue of trust. I never talked about any open investigation for ethical reasons, but this would've been so far beyond that." He paused. "Then the day we executed the arrest warrant, I prayed you wouldn't be at the house. But damn if you didn't open the door. I'll never forget the devastation on your face. Devastation and disgust."

Grace jerked away and stabbed at another box with her key, desperate to squash the memories of that moment. The moment his deception clicked in her brain and slammed her heart to the ground all over again.

"What did you expect?" She took a deep breath to steady the swirling unrest before it could become a full-blown tempest. *Did any of it really matter at this point?* "You know what? Don't answer that. What happened, happened. I think we need to agree to leave the past in the past, and focus on why we're here."

Michael started to say something, then apparently thought better of it. He returned to the box he'd opened, shoulders rigid. "Right," he said, his voice tight. "I gave you the truth, Grace. It's all I've got. You're the only one who can decide if it's enough."

Grace had no answer, so she said nothing. Busting into the last box, she shoved his words into a corner of her heart to examine later when her brain wasn't so clouded. The box contained nothing but old books she'd planned to drop off at a donation center. She shuffled them around to see if there was anything beneath them before finally giving up, worry and defeat hitting her square in the chest. "I think we're done here. We've searched every box."

Michael turned toward the stack of boxes from her apartment. "Not these."

Grace shook her head. "He couldn't have gotten to any of that stuff. Those were everyday items. Dishes. Linens. Some clothes."

"We have to check them."

His tone was firm, but she wondered if he was just stalling, unwilling to admit to their failure. She swallowed her sigh, knowing he was right. They had to know for sure.

"Fine."

After every box had been opened and searched, they came up empty.

"You're sure there's nowhere else to search? Did your mom keep a storage unit?"

"I don't know. I'll have to call her in the morning and ask. She was shell-shocked when it all went down, but it's hard to imagine she'd just toss everything."

Grace's stomach growled, causing Michael's lips to twitch. "Sounds like we better get you some food. And we're done here, anyway. Taco Bell?"

She nodded. "Always good for me."

Michael tried to hide his disappointment in their failure, but it was there in his stance as he stood by the door. Grace folded over the box lids to reseal them as best she could then Michael re-stacked them against the wall.

A couple of books remained on the table. Michael walked over to them and held up a copy of *Fahrenheit 451*. "This was my favorite book in college. I loved the irony that it was a banned book."

The half-smile on his lips as he thumbed through it made Grace's stomach do a little flip. He was giving her the time she needed to think things through, but he looked too damn good for her to think straight. She needed space, yet she walked straight over to him like a magnet.

"Take it," she offered. "I'm not a reader. Truth is, I'd planned to take this box to Goodwill. You want any of the others?" She picked up another book out of the box. "How about *Catcher in the Rye*? I'm sure that was for a book report in high school. I guarantee you I read the Cliff's notes instead, if anything." She shook her head as she glanced at another one. "Probably not this one. *Anne of Green Gables* doesn't really seem like your style."

Seconds ticked by in silence before Michael slowly raised his head. "So, there's no chance you would spend any time perusing your reading collection."

Grace shook her head. "Um. No. I'll listen to an audio book every once in a while, but that's as close as I'm going to get."

In one swift move, Michael upended the box, sending books clattering onto the table.

Grace sucked in a breath. "What are you doing?"

Michael looked at her, eyes bright. "Ernie never expected you to find his secret. Never wanted you to. If he was smart, and he was, he'd put it in the one place he knew you absolutely wouldn't look."

The excitement in Michael's voice compelled her to pick up one of the books, right along with him. "Put what?"

Michael shook his head as he fanned out the pages of *Hamlet* then turned it over, shaking it out. "I don't know. Perry said he had a data backup, so a flash drive maybe?"

Grace followed his lead, and the pile of discarded books grew. With every book they sifted through, her anxiety grew. In her head the countdown had begun. Eight books left, seven, six. She pulled out *Of Mice and Men*, her heart stuttering in her chest when a small manila envelope fell out onto the table. Her hand shook as she scooped it up and held it out to Michael. "Or maybe something like this?"

CHAPTER FOUR

Michael slid a finger under the sealed lip of the envelope and a single key slipped into his palm. Excitement thrummed through his veins as he fished out a piece of paper with BOX 231 hand-written on it.

"Well, hell." He rolled the key in his palm. "Safe deposit box key, but no idea which bank it belongs to."

"That's definitely Ernie's writing, though. You can bet he knew the bank, and that was all that mattered," Grace added.

Michael nodded, wishing he could soothe the worry on her face. Finding the key compounded their problems because it would take time they didn't have to find out where it belonged, but it was better than turning up a goose egg. He just hoped like hell it meant something.

His phone buzzed in his pocket, the caller's name forcing Michael into a decision he'd hoped to delay. "Give me one second." He stepped away from Grace then answered the phone. "Venetti."

"Where are you?" Frustration edged Brian's voice.

Michael hesitated. "I'm with Grace. What's up?"

"I came by your place to talk to her, and I wasn't the first person looking for her here."

Michael's sense of urgency grew, but knowing that Grace was safe with him kept him from overreacting. "Shit. What's the damage?"

"Front door was busted open when I got here, so I came on in. Everything's trashed, man."

Michael twitched. Not many people knew Grace was with him. Or where he lived. Although, it wouldn't take long for a motivated person to figure it out. He squeezed the key tight in his hand, and went with his gut.

"Thanks for the heads up. We'll find a room for the night. I'll be in touch."

"I'm not reporting this. The last thing we need is anyone poking around, asking questions."

"Understood."

"But she knows something, Michael. They're convinced of it, so I am, too." His voice hardened. "Don't let her play you."

Michael bit his tongue to keep the wrong words from spilling out. "I won't."

He shoved the phone back into his pocket as Grace stepped toward him.

"You clench that jaw any tighter, you're going to break it. What happened?"

He released a breath. Protecting Grace was more important than anything else, and that meant full disclosure. "That was Perry on the phone. My place is trashed."

Her face drained of color. "What?"

Michael pulled her into his side. "Come on." He looked around the small space. "Anything here you can wear? We need to lay low for a few days."

Grace rallied as she pulled clothes from a box, then found a tote bag in another and shoved everything in. "I'm ready. So, what's the plan?"

After closing her car door, Michael scanned the quiet night then slid into the driver's seat. "The plan is to keep you safe while we figure out where this key belongs."

"After Taco Bell."

"After Taco Bell," he agreed.

They made quick work of their food, but Grace had gone quiet for the last several blocks. As the tension in the car heightened, Michael waited. He knew better than to force the conversation.

A few minutes later, she twisted toward him. "They came after you." Her voice was subdued. "I've barely wrapped my head around it at all, but I didn't think about you being in danger because of Ernie. Because of me." She paused. "You should take me in. I want you to take me in."

Grace's quiet words deepened Michael's frown as he shot her a sideways glance. "No way in hell."

"I don't want you risking your life for mine." Her voice rose. "I don't want that weight on me."

His grip tightened on the steering wheel as he accelerated to hit highway speed, headed north. "Not a discussion I'm willing to have."

"Why didn't you tell Perry about the key? Do you not trust him?"

The weight of her gaze pressed on Michael as he considering how to answer. It was something he'd asked himself. "I thought I did. But he's on a short list of people who know what's going on, and I don't like convenient coincidences. I want a chance to get everything lined up, so there aren't any more mistakes, or any more deaths."

"You told him we're headed to a hotel. If you think he's involved, it wouldn't be hard for him to use your card to track us down, right?"

"I told him we would get a room tonight. I never said anything about a hotel."

Grace's brow furrowed. "Then where are we going?"

Michael's eyes didn't leave the road. "Door County. The cabin."

The Eighties XM station provided the soundtrack as the suburban sprawl faded in Grace's side mirror, giving way to open highway in front of them. She wanted to ask questions about what was next, but the look on Michael's face in the blue light of the dashboard was one she remembered well. Gears were definitely turning in that intelligent brain of his.

She'd been off-kilter for the past hour, ever since Michael had ripped a hole in her heart. Despite everything else that had happened tonight, much of her heart and mind had been preoccupied with the declaration that he still loved her. A tiny part of her grabbed those words and drank them in like a dying flower.

Was she insane? Did she really want to open the door to heartache all over again? All she knew was that the thought of Michael being in danger sent her sideways. And that being with him made her feel more alive than she had in months. And where did that leave her?

She sighed deeply as they pulled off the highway and made their way to the small cabin Michael had built with his father eight or nine years ago. On the water, the setting had been idyllic for making the memories that flooded her mind. Summer weekends fishing and biking. Winter weekends where snow had kept her snuggled next to Michael in front of the stone fireplace.

He parked in the gravel drive. Grace climbed out of the car then followed the meandering path to the front door, enjoying the late summer aroma of the lilies. Michael came up next to her and she eyed the backpack on his shoulder. "You seriously had a bag packed already?"

He grinned. "What can I say? A good Boy Scout always has a bug-out bag ready."

Light flooded the simple living room after Michael flipped the switch and stepped aside. "Ladies first," he said with a gallant sweep of his arm.

Grace rolled her eyes as she walked in. "Funny, I don't remember you playing the gentleman here before."

Memories of their times at the cabin kept her smiling. Carefree times, full of love and laughter. And the hottest sex she'd ever had. Times when she had no desire for him to be a gentleman.

She pivoted on her heel, and the look on Michael's face told her he knew exactly what she was implying. "Sorry. That was out of line."

He stepped toward her, and she suddenly felt very much like a rabbit in a trap. Her legs decided to quit moving.

"No take-backs at the cabin," Michael whispered.

The history behind those silly words forced Grace to blink back tears. He'd said them the first time she'd told him she loved him. Eyes darkening, his hand slid to her hip and she let him pull her close, until there was barely an inch between them. She held her breath waiting to see what he would do, and damning herself for it.

Michael leaned down, his lips grazing hers, silently asking for permission. And she was lost. She was done fighting the physical attraction, and the yearning in her heart that consumed her when she was with him.

His tongue darted out, skimming her lips, coercing them open. He groaned as her mouth opened for him, his arm tightening behind her, drawing her into contact with the heat of his body.

Grace pulled back, placing her fingertips over his mouth, the tears that had threatened spilling down her cheeks. "Don't hurt me, Michael."

The remorse in his eyes melted whatever resistance she'd had in reserve. His hand closed around her wrist as he placed a soft kiss against her fingers. Then he pulled her in tight, his lips in her hair. "Never again. I promise."

She closed her eyes, reveling in the sweet moment. She wanted to believe him. Wanted to forget everything bad and get lost here, now, with him.

Her free hand snaked through his thick hair and that was all it took for him to lose control. His lips crashed down on hers, and it was as if they'd never been apart. Their bodies knew each other intimately.

Every touch, every pressure point was magnified. His hand captured her breast, tweaking her nipple as he swallowed her moan of pleasure.

"Forgive me, Grace," he whispered against her lips. "Let me love you."

"I do. I have." Her tongue circled his lips then delved into his mouth as months of hurt and sadness ebbed away.

She reached between them and found the button of his jeans, and the suppressed power raging against it. The denim barrier was no match for her wandering hands. Michael moaned low in his throat, then broke the kiss.

"I'm five seconds away from losing control."

Grace squeezed him. "Five…four…"

He scooped her into his arms. "Three," he growled, marching to the bedroom. "Two." He lowered her to her feet. "One," he whispered, then stripped her t-shirt from her.

Her breasts strained against her lace bra, aching for his strong grip. But his touch was light against her neck, her shoulders, her arms. Almost reverent. She closed her eyes, content for the moment to let him have control.

"God, you're so beautiful," he whispered, the breath from his words fanning out across her chest a second before his mouth closed around her straining nipple. His hands held her hips in place as he sucked first one then the other.

Her hands tangled in his hair, encouraging him, without words, to hurry. He answered her plea by releasing the button on her jeans and sliding them down over her hips. Without hesitation, his fingers found their way around her panties to the spot that begged for his touch. His teasing motions sent her careening over the edge. Chest heaving, she pulled his head up to meet her lips, panting into his open mouth. "I want you inside me."

"Thought you'd never ask," he whispered, seconds before his lips crushed hers.

His lowered her to the bed, then played her body with hands that teased the inside of her thighs and her abdomen, his light touch sending a shower of pleasure through her. Coiled tight, she was ready as he settled over her. He paused, his lips dancing with hers once more before he entered her, hard and deep.

Electricity rocketed through her with the first stroke and the next and the next, driving her mad as she clamped ever tighter around his raging cock.

"Grace," he grated, then tendons in his neck straining against his need. "Come with me."

Her eyes slid closed, forgetting everything except the building pressure inside her. Time stopped as her world was once again consumed by the only man she'd ever loved. Her release was followed shortly by his, then he collapsed on the bed next to her, his labored breathing matching hers.

Michael pulled Grace against him, his body sated for the moment. His mind traced back the miracle of the last thirty minutes, to the indelible image of Grace's face when she accepted his apology. And for the first time since he'd walked away from her, the broken, empty place in his heart didn't ache.

Her quiet, even breathing infiltrated his thoughts. It had been a running joke between them how quickly she fell asleep after sex, but right now he had no desire to tease her about it. He had every desire to start their life over again.

Thoughts of the house, and the renovations they would make drifted through his head. They'd sought that property as much for themselves as to flip it, but would she still want to live there? Or would memories of the intruder and the vandalism wreck that possibility?

As quietly as he could, Michael slid away from Grace and shoved into his jeans. None of their future plans were possible until they were out from under this case.

The bedroom door squeaked in protest as he pulled it partially closed it behind him. The old desktop computer his mom had brought over last time they upgraded would now come in handy. He rarely went anywhere without his laptop, but at this point, there was a good chance it was either smashed or stolen.

While the system went through its updates, he wandered to the kitchen and grabbed a bottle of water, his mind shifting gears to Brian. He'd led the team on the original money laundering case, and Michael had been impressed by his instincts and how he'd handled the case. So, what was different now? Was it just the fact that Grace was involved and in danger?

Michael shook his head. It wasn't necessarily a matter of trust. He just needed to control as many of the variables as possible. Settling in at the desk, he pulled up a Google search bar to get suggestions on the fastest, easiest way to locate the bank associated with the key.

With his plan in place, he leaned back in the leather chair, hands clasped behind his head. A creak in the floorboard behind him had him reaching for his hip before he realized he'd left his gun in the bedroom. He swiveled in the chair and breathed a silent sigh of relief as Grace, looking beautifully sleep-tousled, walked toward him then straddled his lap.

She placed her hands on his cheeks, her eyes searching his. "You okay?"

Thoughts of the case flew out of his head as he pulled her close, his lips finding hers. She melted against him, sending a straight shot of lust to his groin. In one fluid motion, he rose and she wrapped her legs around his waist as her lips trailed his jawline.

He kicked the bedroom door closed behind them, his hands squeezing the sweet roundness of her ass as he stalked toward the bed. "Ask me in an hour."

CHAPTER FIVE

Grace blinked against the morning sunshine filtering through the sheer curtains then checked her phone for the time. Make that almost afternoon sunshine. She rolled over toward Michael, struck again by the fact that she was in his bed, and he was back in her life.

She traced the planes of his face, a face she could now admit she'd missed desperately. She leaned in and kissed his forehead. "You going to sleep the day away?" she whispered.

His eyes opened, a slow smile on his lips. "Not with you next to me." He stretched and she couldn't help enjoying the long lean contours of his body, accentuated by the cream-colored sheet covering him.

When her eyes returned to his, the heat she saw there sent butterflies racing through her. She pulled the sheet down, her mouth seeking his hard nipple while her fingers went lower, circling and stroking.

"God, I've missed you."

His graveled voice turned her on as much as the body that shuddered under her hands. His possessive fingers threaded through her hair, forcing her mouth to his for a kiss that ignited the fire smoldering inside her.

He effortlessly flipped their positions, his pelvis rocking against the barrier of her panties. Pressure and frustration drove her hips to respond. "No more teasing," she pleaded.

He had mercy on her, removing her panties then filling her until she thought she would burst with the pleasure. Once again, she lost her mind as he exploded inside her, his final thrusts propelling her over the edge with him.

Michael gathered her into his arms, his fingers absently playing along her abdomen beneath the swell of her breasts.

She burrowed into his side. "Fair warning. You do that much longer, and I'm going to need you to touch me in other places."

"I'll touch you in any place you want," Michael replied, without a hint of apology for his wandering hands. "But since you kept me up all night, literally, I may need a few minutes."

"I kept you up?" Grace teased. "I seem to remember –"

"Or however that worked out." He squeezed her ribcage before shoving off the bed. "Either way, you are too tempting. And as much as I'd like to do nothing but stay in this room all day with you, duty calls."

The shadow of the case was there, but she equated the cabin with safety, insulated from the rest of the world, off the beaten path. Her smile dipped a bit knowing he was heading back to Chicago, but he seemed confident in this next step.

She sat up in the bed. "You think your father's friend will be able to help us?"

"I don't know. I hope so."

"What if he can't?"

Michael walked over to her side of the bed and planted a kiss on her lips. "Then we find another solution."

His assurance helped quell the anxiety building in her chest. With a nod, she whipped off the sheet and kneeled on the bed. Her hands framed his face and she kissed him once, hard. "Okay."

He pulled her against the hardness of his chest, then released her. "I need to call Mr. Chaffee. Make sure he's in town. When you're ready, we'll grab a few things from the store before I head back."

He'd flipped the mental switch, his mind already gearing toward the work he needed to do, a pattern so familiar to her it seemed as if they'd never really been apart.

"Go ahead and go. It's already almost noon. I can bike into town to grab what we need."

He frowned. "Not sure I like that idea."

She shrugged. "I could use the fresh air and exercise. And we're safe here." She swatted his wandering hands. "Now, go on so I can get dressed without your interference."

He helped her off the bed. "I forgot how bossy you are."

She attempted to swat his ass as he walked away but he sidestepped, his laughter following him out of the room. Grace shook her head as she found something suitable to wear for her ride.

By the time she worked her hair into a French braid, Michael had reached Mr. Chaffee and had gotten permission to come by. He strode over to her and stole her breath with a kiss before heading out.

Michael hit the open highway, the periodic road construction adding to his frustration with the clock. In truth, getting back to Chicago should've been his first priority today. If Mr. Chaffee could use his experience to tell Michael which banks used the type of key that was tucked in Michael's pocket, it would save them time in the long run. But there was no way

Michael would regret how he'd spent the last twelve hours.

Grace had forgiven him.

He let that truth wash over him again. Miles flew by as the hope that had sprung to life last night had time to translate into visions of the future he thought he'd lost. The ring she'd mailed back to him had worn grooves in his wallet. He wanted it back on her finger. Soon.

The buzz of his cell phone from the cup holder interrupted his musings. He frowned at the precinct number on the screen. "Venetti."

Captain Evans was on the phone. "You got some time to come in today? Marti called this morning. Her doctor put her on bedrest until the baby comes and we need to divvy up her cases."

"I'm actually taking a couple of personal days myself." Timing sucked, but Michael had no choice.

"Well, shit. That's news to me. When did that happen?"

"Yesterday."

The captain paused. "That's kind of sudden. Everything good?"

"Absolutely." Michael smiled. "Reconnecting with a friend."

Papers shuffled in the background. "There's nothing earth-shattering here, but we can't let this stuff pile up. What about your car thieves? That one about finished?"

"Just about. Waiting on some follow-ups from two other municipalities to make sure we lock them down for good."

"I'll have Jason give you a call later so he can get the skinny. You back next week?"

I hope so. "Yep."

Michael hung up the phone and turned into his old neighborhood. Dale Chaffee lived a couple of blocks over from his parents' house. Guilt niggled because he wasn't going to stop to see them, but they'd have twenty questions that Michael couldn't or wouldn't answer. Plus, he needed to get back to the cabin. Grace had texted him that she returned safely from town, but he'd feel much better when she was back in his arms.

He turned into Mr. Chaffee's driveway and there was no mistaking the man trimming the rosebush by the front door. He was smaller than Michael remembered, but the sparkle in his eyes as he set the trimmers on the porch and walked over was exactly the same.

"Well, if it isn't little Mikey Venetti."

Michael extended his hand and instead was wrapped in a full hug, stronger than he'd expected. "Thanks for letting me stop by on short notice."

"Of course. What's it been? Ten, twelve years or more? Hell, it's probably been six dadgum months since I've seen your folks. Time gets away when you get to be my age." He opened the front door and led

Michael to a linen covered dining table. "Fran should be back from the store shortly. I promised I'd keep you here until she got back."

He poured Michael a glass of iced tea then motioned him to sit on one of the slip-covered chairs. "Sounds like detective work's keeping you busy."

"That it is."

Dale sat down at the head of the table and extended his hand. "All right then. Let's take a look at that key."

Michael produced the key from his pocket, waiting patiently as the older man slipped on his glasses and looked it over.

"I take it you're looking for the owner?"

"Not exactly. I know who the owner is. I'm looking for the bank this key belongs to."

Letting out a low whistle, Dale perched his glasses in his thinning white hair and handed the key back to Michael. "Well, my boy. I have good news and bad news. Good news is that this is a Diebold key. Easy to identify. Bad news is, they're a popular manufacturer. Back before I retired, several of the banks in the area used them. I'm assuming they still do."

Michael blew out a breath. "I was afraid you were going to say that. We're in a time crunch. Any suggestions on where to start looking?"

Dale thought for a minute. "I'd start with US Bank of the Heartland. They have quite a few branches, but they're probably your odds-on favorite.

I seem to remember drilling open quite a few boxes for them over the years, so I know they do a decent lockbox business."

Mrs. Chaffee arrived in time to send Michael off with a hug and a tin of homemade sugar cookies. "You tell your mother and father we want to see them over for bridge soon."

"Will do." After another round of hugs, he thanked Dale again and climbed into his car. Michael backed out of their driveway and returned their wave as they stood, arm in arm, on the porch.

He hit the highway smiling. The Chaffees were one of several long, happy marriages he'd witnessed growing up. And while he wasn't in a hurry to grow old, he was in a damn hurry to get this case resolved and get on with his life, with Grace by his side.

Anxious to hear her voice, he dialed her number, relieved all over again when she answered on the second ring.

"Hey. How'd it go?" she asked.

"To quote Mr. Chaffee, I have good news and bad news."

Grace pulled the steaming pan of lasagna from the oven. The aroma of basil and oregano filled the small kitchen, but did little to permeate the fog that had settled over her. Her brilliant idea to make Michael his favorite dinner had backfired big time as worst-case scenarios started creeping into her head. Irrational. Foolish even, when she whispered them out loud. But by the time Michael turned the key in the lock and opened the door, they were absolutely real.

He walked into the kitchen and breathed deep before meeting her in front of the stove with the grin she'd anticipated as she'd wandered the market aisles. He wrapped her in his arms and nodded toward the cheesy garlic bread before nuzzling the sensitive spot where her neck and shoulder met. "I am starving. But I could die a happy man right now just smelling this feast."

His words sent a shiver through her, but as she wiggled away from him to ready their plates, she gave him her best smile. "You have to at least eat it first before you keel over."

"You'll get no argument out of me."

He followed her to the table carrying the basket of bread, and she tried to drown out the anxiety filling her mind. *He's here. He's safe.*

Michael sat down and eyed the candles and fresh flowers. "Wow. What's all this?"

Grace manufactured another smile. "I missed your birthday, so I thought I'd make it up to you."

He forked up a bite of the rich pasta then closed his eyes and moaned. "Damn, babe. Even better than I remember."

Michael kept the conversation going through dinner, but Grace couldn't shake her worries. She made it through the meal without melting down, but she needed to get her head on straight. Maybe a walk down by the water's edge, or even a soak in the tub would help.

Finishing off her glass of merlot, she stood. "Let me take your plate."

Michael stood up with her. "No way. You cooked. I clean. That's the rule." He followed her to the kitchen and set down his plate then reached for Grace's hand.

She tried to pull away, but he wouldn't let go. She shook her head, tears perilously close to the surface.

"Grace?" He squeezed her a little tighter. "Hey. Look at me." She bit her lip and met his gaze. "What's wrong?"

She swallowed hard as two fat tears broke free and trailed down her cheeks. Her free hand tapped against her leg as she swallowed again. She didn't want to have this conversation, but the words tumbled out anyway.

"I don't – I don't know if I can do this," she whispered.

Michael shook his head as a muscle tightened in his jaw. "Do what? I don't understand."

Grace took a deep, shaky breath. "Making dinner." She paused, searching for the right words. "I was here by myself, thinking about what you were doing today and the dangers you face in your job."

"I was talking to a retired locksmith."

She ignored his intentionally obtuse comment. "And the more I thought about it, the more I wondered if I could face the knowledge that any meal could be our last together."

The pressure in her chest continued to build, but Michael blocked her attempt to move around him. He gripped her shoulders, his voice low. "Stop."

"I'm sorry. But, what if some drugged out gangbanger makes a decision that your life isn't worth the ounce of heroin in his back pocket?"

He shook his head. "That's not my life, Grace."

She looked up at him. "Isn't it? Ever?"

"Next to never," he said, his voice rising. "You're being nonsensical. To follow that logic, you should never marry a dog catcher because he could be mauled to death, or a taxi driver because he could die in a car wreck, or a chef because he could cut off his thumb and bleed out."

Grace closed her eyes. Everything he said was true and logical. But this was Michael, not some hypothetical guy. He had her heart. He'd always had it. The past few months, she'd tried so hard to move on, but life was just better with him. Brighter. Night and day.

He pulled her toward the computer desk. "You want to see what ninety-eight percent of my job consists of? Let me show you." He toggled the mouse until the screen sprang to life then ran a Google search for US Bank of the Heartland. "See that? He pointed to the screen. I'm going to pull a list of the branches in the Chicagoland area with addresses and phone numbers. That's the kind of stuff I do. I'll go through every single one until I find what I'm looking for, or don't."

Grace took a calming breath. "I know." She scooted to the left and handed him three printed pages. "It's just the other two percent that freaks me out."

Michael flipped through the list of bank branches, his mouth dropped open. "Well, damn."

His look of surprise forced her first real smile of the evening. Michael pulled her in close and dropped a kiss in her hair. "I won't let you push me away. What we have is too good, too special."

Sagging against him, she wrapped her arms around his waist. "I don't want to, but these thoughts keep crowding out the good."

"Then let's crowd them out." He released her, jogged to the kitchen and returned seconds later. Wine bottle and glasses in hand, he motioned toward the sofa. "Have a seat," he said, kicking off his shoes. "Ugly Truth? Or Maid in Manhattan?"

She laughed out loud. Her favorite silly romantic comedies. Of course he remembered. An hour later, the heaviness Grace had worn diminished. The trifecta of wine, humor and relaxation had all but banished her fears. Michael was a great detective, and a hell of a smart guy. Worrying about things she couldn't control wouldn't help either one of them.

The movie ended and Grace leaned up, brushing his jawline with her lips. "Thanks for talking me off the ledge."

She hopped onto his lap and circled his neck with her arms, her lips meeting his, holding nothing back. She needed this man like she needed to breathe. Within seconds, his shirt was gone, and Grace rained kisses across his neck and shoulders while her hips worked against his.

A vibration against her thigh pulled her brain back to reality. "I think that's you," she whispered, climbing off his lap.

Michael's passion-glazed eyes opened and he stood, fumbling for the phone in his pocket. "Shit. I need to take this." He kissed her hard on the mouth. "We're not finished."

She rose on tiptoes and nipped his ear. "No, we're not."

He groaned then punched the talk button. "Hey, Jason." A pause. "Yep. Captain calls it playing hooky. I call it a couple of days rest and relaxation." Michael's gaze darted to Grace. "Yes. We're good. Better than good."

Grace smiled then picked up the empty wine bottle and glasses and headed to the kitchen to give Michael privacy. She loaded the dishwasher and wiped down the counters, hoping that would give him plenty of time for his call, and give her time to cool her racing heart. But when she returned to the living room, the stoked heat in his eyes as he watched her spread warmth through every nerve in her body.

As she listened for verbal clues that the call was ending, it was obvious from Michael's side of the conversation that the call had moved on from work-related subjects.

Michael grimaced. "A thousand bucks? Yeah, that sucks." Another minute passed. "Guess it wasn't your night."

He held the phone away from his ear and she could hear the monologue through the phone. Grace covered her grin, then decided to have a little fun at Michael's expense. She raised her arms behind her, slowly uncoiling her braid. Eyes locked squarely on her chest, his mock glare encouraged her to take her sweet time. Next, she shook out her hair then undid the buttons of her shirt causing the teasing glint in his eyes to flee.

"Um, yeah. I'm here. Look Jason, I gotta go."

Grace turned her back to let her shirt drop. She looked over her shoulder, realizing a split second too late that Michael had tossed his phone on the couch and was stalking her way.

"You are going to pay for that."

Squealing, Grace tried to bolt but Michael lunged for her, wrapping her up in his arms. "Oh, no you don't. Time to finish what you started."

Grace barely summoned the strength to sit up on the sofa. "That love seat may have to stay in storage. I think we just found its replacement."

Michael barked out a laugh as he pulled her into his side. "Bite your tongue." He planted a kiss on her forehead before getting up and stepping back into his jeans. "Although I appreciate your tactics for getting me off the phone."

Grace forced her languid muscles to move and scooped up her clothes. "You're welcome. He was a talker."

"Try being his desk partner." Michael shook his head. "Ask anyone at the station. Jason Nunez'll talk your ear off. Usually about his trips to the casino or poker night." He walked over to the computer desk and grabbed the list of bank branches. "Thanks for printing these, by the way."

Grace finished the last two buttons on her shirt and followed Michael to the kitchen table. Back to reality, and the daunting task in front of them.

She picked up one of the pages. "Let's pretend we find the right branch. What do we do then? We don't have a death certificate. What are the chances they'll even let us look at the box?"

"That depends on three things. The efforts of my friend Bonnie at the probate office, the experience of the box keeper at the bank, and sheer dumb luck."

Grace gaped at him, shaking her head. *Was he really counting on sheer dumb luck?*

Oh, boy.

CHAPTER SIX

Grace poured a cup of coffee and stepped out the back door into the briskness of the cool September morning. She settled into one of the patio rocking chairs and curled her legs underneath her. This time of year, the weather was not her friend. Although it wasn't quite autumn yet, the temperatures were dropping, and snow might only be a month away.

Today, she'd have to spend some time connecting with her contractors and delaying her project start date. They'd love her for that. But what choice did she have? She rolled her neck, trying not to borrow trouble. And she had a whole bunch of more pressing phone calls to make.

She took a sip from her steaming mug, then closed her gritty eyes. She'd slept like hell last night, tossing and turning, her mind conjuring so many ways the next several days could go wrong. *So much for not worrying.*

"There you are." Michael opened the weathered screen door and walked over to the porch railing, staring out into the gray morning. "Banks should be open in about ten minutes."

Grace set her coffee on the small glass top table then walked over to Michael and wrapped her arms around his middle. He was worried, too. She could feel it in the set of his shoulders.

"I'll call every one of them. All we can do is try. And hope that his box at one of them."

Michael turned in her arms. and rested his chin on her head, squeezing her against him. When he released her, his face was tight and determined. "This will work. It has to. I won't lose you again, Grace."

Grace sat down at the kitchen table with the list, her cell phone, and another cup of coffee. Hopefully, it would calm her nervous stomach. Michael grabbed a jacket from the tree by the door then came back to the table for a quick kiss.

"You're good here?"

"I'll be fine," she nodded. "I'll call you if I have any luck."

"*When* you have luck," he corrected. "My first stop will be the probate office. Even if we don't find the right bank today, we'll need something that's somewhat official either way."

She had qualms about his plan after reading everything she could find online about safety deposit box protocol, but none of it mattered if she didn't get on the phone and find the right damn bank. She grabbed her cell and dialed the first one on the list. After following the automated attendant, she got a live person.

"U.S. Bank of the Heartland."

"Good morning. My name is Grace Cooper." She sat straighter in her chair, trying to project confidence. "My stepfather, Ernie Kinsley, has passed away. He had a safe deposit box with your bank, but we're trying to confirm which branch. Can you tell me if you have a box in his name?"

"My condolences for your loss. Let me transfer you."

Grace waited, her grip on the phone tight. What if they wouldn't disclose the information?

A woman picked up the line. "Good morning. May I help you?"

Grace repeated her request then waited for what seemed like ten minutes.

"I'm sorry. We don't have any boxes registered to that name."

A mixture of disappointment and relief swept through her. It might take a while to figure out which location, but at least the bank was willing to give her information. Assuming she was calling the right bank. But even if she wasn't, she'd call every freaking bank in Chicago to get answers.

She drew a line through the eleventh branch then took a short bathroom break and toasted a bagel. By the time she finished it off between calls, she was well onto page two and her confidence was waning. She arched her back to stretch her scrunched shoulders and dialed the next number on the list, reciting again the words she said countless times already.

"Yes, ma'am," the man replied. "Ernest Kinsley. Box was opened last December."

Grace almost dropped her phone, her brain working feverishly to do a course correction and not sound like a complete idiot. "Oh. Um. Box 231?"

"Yes, ma'am. Wait. Is this the same Ernest Kinsley who was just –," he paused. "I'm sorry. Never mind."

Buzzing with excitement, Grace ignored the curiosity in the man's voice. "Thank you so much." Her hand was shaking so much she almost dropped her phone when she hit the end button. Jumping out of her chair, she fist-pumped the air. "Yes!"

She dialed Michael's number and paced until he answered.

"Hey, babe."

"Michael," she breathed. "We got it. We got it! His box is at the Crystal Lake branch." She rattled off the address for him. "How long until you can get there?"

"You're a rock star. Okay. I'm about thirty minutes out of the city. I talked to Bonnie and she's got me covered, so even with traffic I should be to Crystal Lake in an hour, hour fifteen."

"Call me as soon as you know something."

She needed to make the calls to her contractors, but she was going to be worthless until she heard back from Michael. Instead, she used her nervous energy to scour the cabin, cleaning every surface until it shone.

A knock sounded at the front door, and Grace glanced at the clock, dropping the blanket she was folding onto the bed. Michael had barely had time to get to the bank, which meant he was still hours away. There were homes on either side of the cabin, but she had no idea who lived there, or whether they were full-time or seasonal residents.

She approached the solid wood door, wishing there was a peephole. Heart in her throat, she placed a hand on the doorknob.

"Who's there?"

"Grace?" A pause. "I'm Detective Jason Nunez. Michael's partner. Last night, he asked me to run some paperwork up here to him. Is he around?"

Grace breathed a sigh of relief and swung the door open, instantly recognizing the man's face from the day they came to arrest Ernie. "I'm sorry, but he's not here."

"Ah, man. Don't tell me he headed back to Chicago. I could've met him there."

Grace grimaced. "He did." She extended her arm and motioned him in. "I hate to think you wasted the entire drive. I can't imagine what he was thinking. Can I at least offer you a cup of coffee?"

Detective Nunez chuckled as he stepped over the threshold. "I'd sure appreciate it."

"Of course, come on in." She walked to the kitchen and readied the pot. "Have a seat. This won't take more than a couple minutes."

She turned toward him to place mugs on the table, but he wasn't sitting. He was standing against the wall, pointing his pistol straight at her chest.

"Don't hurry on my account. I'm not leaving without seeing you both."

Michael walked into the small bank lobby, controlled energy thrumming through his veins, his brain one hundred percent focused on gaining access to whatever information Ernie had.

The place was quiet for a Monday early afternoon, the only customer an older woman filling out paperwork to his right. He approached the teller.

"Hi there. I need to speak to someone about a safe deposit box."

She hopped off her stool. "Oh, sure. One second. Randy's your guy."

Michael watched as she walked toward the drive-thru and spoke to a man in his early twenties who looked like he enjoyed the gym. He finished up with his customer then walked toward Michael.

"Good afternoon. How can I help you today?"

"I need access to a safe deposit box. Number 231. Registered to Ernest Kinsley."

A slight frown puckered Randy's brow. "I talked to a woman earlier today about that. His stepdaughter, I think?"

"Yes. I'm here on her behalf." Michael took out his badge and slid it forward on the counter. "Detective Michael Venetti."

Michael released a slow breath as he waited. He wasn't going to say another word until he knew what avenue he needed to take.

Randy's eyes lit up. "Wait. I know you."

Of all the things the kid could've said, that one took Michael by surprise. "Yeah?"

"I'm a part-time student at McHenry County Community College. Studying criminology. I saw the YouTube video of the shooting outside the courthouse. I've followed that case for a while now."

Michael hated the fact that the world had devolved to a state of near-constant recording. But today, it played to his favor. "That was a tough day."

He checked his watch. "The investigation is ongoing, which is why I'm here."

Randy glanced back toward the drive-thru window. Indecision warred on his face. "I think I have to wait for a bank officer –"

Michael offered a reassuring smile and pulled out the letter from the probate office. It wasn't exactly a court order, but he was hoping Randy didn't look too close. "I'm here with permission from the family and the court. And I'm pressed for time today."

Eyes darted to the paper then back at Michael. "And you have the key?"

"I do."

One more look over his shoulder. "Hey, Allison? Can you handle everything for a few minutes while I run him back?"

She waved him on. "No problem."

Randy stepped to his left and opened a swinging gate for Michael. "This way."

Michael sensed Randy's hesitation, so he kept up a steady stream of conversation about the young man's career plans as he walked next to him. This kid was all that stood between him and the contents of the box.

Randy took Michael's key then opened a door to a small viewing room. "Have a seat. I'll be right back."

An eternity passed as Michael waited. He leaned back in the chair and crossed his legs instead of pacing the small room. He had no doubt he was being surveilled. Finally, the door opened and Randy walked in, alone, and placed the box on the table.

"I'm required to stay in here with you."

Michael nodded. "That's fine."

Before Michael even opened the lid, Randy stepped forward. "I referenced this case for a paper I wrote on white collar crime last semester. Got an A."

The eagerness in his voice kept Michael from a sharp reply. "It's an interesting case."

Michael opened the metal lid, not surprised to find a single flash drive in a Ziploc bag. No papers. No details. Just the drive. Impatience riffed through him. He'd hoped to lay eyes on something that would give him a measure of certainty that this drive had the data he was after.

He stood and looked hard at Randy. "I'm going to have to take this and enter it as evidence."

Randy had every authority in the world to refuse his request. Michael offered up a silent prayer that he didn't exercise it.

"You think it's tied to the case?"

Michael shrugged, and Randy gave him a knowing look. "I understand. You can't say, right?"

Michael didn't wait for Randy to agree or disagree. Ignoring the small prick at his conscience for bending the rules, he pocketed the drive and opened the door to the room. "You've been really helpful today."

Randy beamed. "Who knows? Maybe someday we'll work a case together."

Michael smiled his response. He wouldn't be opposed. He owed this kid one hell of a favor.

Michael drove back toward Chicago, trying to decide how to check the contents of the drive. It might contain nothing more than personal information, or maybe nothing at all. Ernie was slick. It was possible he'd been playing the FBI.

Returning to the cabin wasted precious time. His laptop was most likely gone or trashed from the break-in, and he couldn't hit the station without a million questions from his captain. Only one good option remained.

He punched in Brian's cell number and waited through three rings before he picked up. "Venetti here. Where are you?"

"I'm at the office. Why? What's up?"

"Stay there. I'll be there in thirty minutes."

"Why do I get the feeling this isn't a social call?"

"Because I don't have time for them, and neither do you." Michael paused. "I think I may have found what we're looking for."

"No shit."

"I'll explain when I get there."

Michael barely made it two steps into the FBI office when Brian approached and rushed him through security. "Let's go to my office."

By the time the elevator dinged at the tenth floor, Michael had filled Brian in on his tactics to retrieve the flash drive.

Brian waved the comments away. "I'm not worried about that right now. If there's information we can use, we'll figure that out. This is Ernie's data, and we have the support of his family to access it."

They walked out of the elevator and down the hall to the last door on the right. "All right, let's see what we've got." Brian inserted the flash drive into the USB port and tapped his foot, waiting for the virus scan to complete. Michael stood behind his right shoulder as more than a hundred files populated the folder.

Oh yeah, they had something.

The first dozen were .wav files with nothing but dates for file names. Brian clicked on the first one then grinned over his shoulder as he hovered over the pop-up message. "Do we trust the source of the file?"

Michael shook his head. "Not any farther than I could've thrown him. But let's hear it."

Ernie's booming voice filled the room, and Brian rushed to turn the volume down on his speakers. As he clicked through all the .wav files, neither of them spoke. Michael could barely believe his ears as he listened to phone conversations between Ernie and a host of influencers, each of whom he was smart enough to name by name on the call. Every call was more stunning than the last. Ernie had coordinated extortions, bribes, payoffs and more for everyone from Senator Barrett, the senior senator from Illinois, down to Michael's own police commissioner and captain.

The silence after the last file played was deafening. Brian looked at Michael, his face reflecting Michael's bewildered thoughts. "Well, I'll be damned," he said quietly. "And look at this." He pointed to the other file types on the drive. "What do you want to bet those are all support docs. Ernie wasn't stupid."

"Yeah." Michael blew out a breath. He'd been sucker punched hearing his own captain's voice on the call. He'd worked under Captain Evans for most of his career. Mind spinning, he replayed yesterday's conversation. Had it really been to talk about case load? Jason had seemed surprised when Michael mentioned Marti's upcoming absence for the baby.

Brian picked up the receiver from his desk. "Patti, get a transcriber up to my office please. Stat." He hung up and looked at Michael. "We have a hell of a lot of work to do."

"You've got to get a massive team on this," Michael urged. "This has to go down fast."

"It will. I'm going to pull every available resource. Starting right now."

Michael nodded, relieved by the sincerity and determination in Brian's eyes. "Grace isn't safe until you have every single one of these bastards. Until then, I need your help to get her relocated."

Brian clapped Michael on the back and shook his hand. "Consider it done."

CHAPTER SEVEN

Grace's heart rate spiked as her brain struggled to make sense of what was happening. Jason was Michael's friend. A police officer. And his hand didn't even tremble a little as Grace stared at the barrel of the gun he had pointed at her.

"What are you doing?" She back-pedaled until her spine pressed against the kitchen counter. "I don't understand."

Jason shifted the barrel toward one of the kitchen chairs. "Have a seat, Grace."

She stood where she was, frozen in place until his dark gaze returned to her face.

"Now."

Her legs trembled, but she complied. It was better to keep him calm, play by his rules.

He quickly secured her wrists to the sides of the chair with zip ties then, thankfully, returned his gun to his holster. She tracked his movements as he poured a cup of coffee then joined her at the table, his bouncing leg adding to her anxiety.

She frowned at him as he took a sip, her mind still coming up empty. "Does this have to do with Michael? I told you he's not here."

"Indirectly. I tried to tell him chasing after you was a bad idea, but he didn't listen. This whole thing could've gone a whole lot easier if he'd fucking listened to me."

Grace shook her head. "What thing?"

"Why is Michael back in Chicago, Grace?"

The hardness in his eyes belied his conversational tone, and his casual use of her first name unnerved her.

"Working?"

Jason shook his head as his grip on the mug tightened. His smile didn't come close to reaching his eyes. "You can do better than that."

Grace's mind raced as she twisted her wrists against the strips of plastic, but no clever answer came to mind. "He's looking for information."

"Yes." Jason nodded as if he already knew the answer. "Do you know what he's looking for?"

She shook her head and he stood so abruptly, she rocked back in her seat.

A muscle in his jaw ticked as he stared down at her. "Don't make this harder than it has to be." He stepped back and took a breath. "I'm going to move my car. Thanks to Michael, this is going to take longer than it should. When I get back, you need to have a different answer."

The front door clicked closed and Grace blinked back hot tears. She tried to get to her feet. If she could get to her phone charging on the counter, she could call Michael. Or 911. Somebody who could help her.

There was no way to stand, and she was sweating by the time she'd scooted the chair to the counter. Her hair fell in her face as she tried to pull the phone off the charger with her teeth. She got it disconnected from the cord and used her nose to switch to the call screen when the front door opened then closed. Her breath froze in her chest. All she had to do was hit the emergency call button.

Heavy footsteps came up short in the kitchen doorway. Jason's eyes narrowed as he realized her intention. With more force than necessary, he yanked her chair back from the counter and palmed her phone. He scanned the screen then tossed it back on the counter.

"You're a very lucky woman," he said between clenched teeth. "If you'd made that call, you'd be dead right now."

Blinding pain ripped through Grace's head as the blow to her jaw jerked her whole body sideways. The coppery taste of blood filled her mouth. She'd never been struck before. Not really. Not like this. Maybe a few times by her sister growing up. Her eyes drifted closed, but she forced them open, focusing on the red and purple flowers on the table.

Jason stood over her. "Don't be that stupid again."

She spit on the floor then nodded, full awareness returning slowly as the shock faded. Grace worked her jaw from side to side, relieved that it wasn't shattered.

"Now that I have your attention, let's start over." Jason took a seat across the table. "Tomorrow I have an appointment with one of the biggest sharks in Chicago. He's going to ask me if I have his hundred grand." His leg began to bounce. "Until a couple days ago, I had no fucking answer. You get that? Nothing. Then, like an angel, you came along. The answer to my prayers." His grin was almost a sneer as he leaned in, the coffee smell on his breath stale in her face. "I don't know how to make this any clearer, Grace. So I'll ask you one more time. Where is Michael and what, exactly, is he after?"

Grace shifted in her seat under his intense scrutiny. He was going to kill them both. It was there in his eyes, the desperation behind the anger. There was no way the truth would satisfy him.

Michael jogged to his car in the underground garage, anxious to cover the miles between him and Grace. As soon as he got above ground, he punched in her number. After four rings, the call went to voicemail.

He reined in his disappointment and waited until he was out of Chicago traffic before he tried again. But once again it went to voicemail. His thumb tapped a quick staccato on the steering wheel. Coverage wasn't great at the cabin, but they hadn't had this kind of trouble connecting yesterday.

Miles and miles filled with mental placating didn't help his overactive imagination. Why wasn't she answering? He started to call her again when a text came through from her.

Sorry I missed you. Getting ready to shower. Hurry back.

Michael let out a breath and some of his pent-up anxiety. He set the phone down, assuming she'd call him back after her shower. But when an hour passed, and he still hadn't heard from her, the alarm bells in his head refused to be silenced. He knew Grace. She would be champing at the bit to know what he'd discovered.

He tried her a couple more times then received another text about an hour from the cabin, which only heightened his worry. She could text, but she couldn't talk? No way.

Starting dinner. How close are you?

Michael spoke his reply. "Probably ninety minutes out. Can you make lasagna? Haven't had it in forever."

A few minutes later his phone dinged.

Absolutely

The single word reply made his heart drop to his stomach. Michael mashed down the accelerator, hoping there were no speed traps set up on this section of Highway 57. Whoever he was communicating with, it wasn't Grace. Time crawled, but he made the remainder of the drive in sixty-five minutes, every mile praying she was safe.

At the last corner before turning onto Bayshore Drive, Michael pulled his car off the shoulder and cut the lights. He reviewed his texts then sent another message. "Thirty minutes out."

Michael shoved his phone in his pocket, thankful for the thick tree cover as he approached the cabin on foot. Senses heightened, he waited near the edge of the property, looking and listening for anything out of place.

Soft waves lapped at the tiny slip of beach behind the house. A bird whistled from somewhere above his head. He frowned. In the soft late-afternoon glow, there should've at least been a light on in the kitchen.

Michael crept toward the back of the house and chanced a look through the small gap in the bedroom curtains. Drawers had been dumped and the mirror over the chest of drawers smashed. *God, let Grace be okay.* He closed his eyes and released a slow breath.

He avoided the creaky board on the back porch then looked in the kitchen window. Grace sat slumped over in a chair, unmoving, blood at her feet.

Michael clamped down on the cold fury and fear that washed over him. As quietly as possible, he pulled the keys from his pocket then slid through the back door into the shadowed room, pistol ready. His eyes adjusted and he did a quick sweep before dropping to Grace's side. With a sick pit in his stomach, he lifted her drooped head, scared to death of what he would see.

He burned with rage at the purpling bruises under her eye and along her jaw. But the steady rise and fall of her chest kept him from losing it completely. Grace opened her eyes, and despite the depth of pain there, he knew she recognized him. The next second, she jerked her head and screamed.

"Michael. Run!"

He reacted instantly, rolling to his side. Instead of the full body blow he anticipated, his shoulder took the brunt of the hit. His attacker stumbled behind him. Michael sprang to his feet and stood in front of Grace, his pistol trained on the man as he slowly rose.

"Jason?"

In the moment it took for Michael to reconcile the truth that his partner was now his enemy, Jason turned with the twin to Michael's Glock raised and ready. "I didn't want to do this." His voice broke. "You're like a brother to me."

Michael almost choked on his anger. "Then why?"

Jason's eyes hardened. "No choice. I'm out of time. I've got to know if Ernie really had anything. Now."

"Anything on who, Jason? Captain Evans? The Commissioner? Which one turned you?"

Eyes wide, Jason's throat worked but he didn't speak. Michael exhaled and pushed back against the darkness that made him want to pull the fucking trigger. "Put the gun down, Jason. They'll never deliver on whatever they promised you. It's over."

Jason remained still as a statue, and Michael remained ready for an attack. But he slowed and softened his tone. "It's over," he repeated. "Not only did I find it, the FBI has it. Perry and his men are issuing subpoenas, and I guarantee you every one of those fuckers is going to prison."

Jason frowned at Michael's words. He blinked twice, then shook his head. "I wish there had been another way. I – I'm sorry. For everything."

He raised the gun to his temple and pulled the trigger before Michael could react. The sound of the gunshot blasted through the small room, followed by Grace's screaming sobs. Michael dug out his pocketknife and fell to his knees to remove her wrist restraints. She collapsed into his arms.

"Oh, my God. Thank God. I was so afraid he'd ambush you."

Michael tried not to hold her too tightly for fear of unseen injuries. His heartbeat pounded in his ears. "You were afraid for *me*? Jesus. I got your texts, but they weren't you. I couldn't let my mind go there." He shuddered then pulled back and examined her face more closely. "God, babe. What did he do to you?"

Her cries into his shoulder were his only answer. Michael struggled to contain converging emotions as his gaze landed on the lifeless body of a man he'd trusted with his life. Anger. Sadness. Guilt. "I didn't protect you. God, Grace. I'm so sorry."

Finally, spent, she pushed away from him. "What are you talking about? You saved my life."

Michael shuddered again as he called 911, unable to contemplate the alternative.

Grace rubbed at the gauze around her wrists as she waited for her release paperwork. The staff at the small regional medical center had been kind, but she was ready to get out of there. They'd confirmed that her injuries would all heal, but the doctors had insisted she stay overnight because of a mild concussion. Michael's stricken face convinced her to agree.

The door squeaked open and he stepped into the room, her Mountain Dew in hand.

She smiled. "Thank you."

His answering smile didn't reach his eyes. He picked up the rumpled blanket he'd used last night off the floor and tossed it on the chair then returned to her bedside.

He jammed his hands in his jeans pockets. "Just got off the phone with Perry. His people will be here within the hour."

Grace frowned. "What? Why?"

Michael looked everywhere but at her. "Until this is finished, you're still in danger. They have a place set up for you."

Her breath caught in her throat. He was sending her away. "I won't go without you."

"It'll only be for a few months."

His rationalization was a lie she refuted. "I'm not going anywhere without you."

Michael ran a hand through his hair, guilt etched on his face. "You'll be safer this way."

A tear leaked down her cheek, but her voice strengthened. "No."

He finally looked at her. "Grace," he whispered, agony in that single word. "I all but promised you there wasn't any danger, and now you're lying there. And I'm standing here." He swallowed hard. "I didn't protect you."

It was the same litany he'd repeated since yesterday. "So you want to send me away. Away from you."

Michael's head bobbed. "At least for now."

"And then what, Michael?" She glared through her one open eye, her tears forgotten as she threw his words back in his face. "Should I just go on? Marry a dogcatcher, maybe? Or a taxi driver?" Her voice rose. "Or how about a chef? Think that will keep me safe?"

"Saf*er*," he cried, his grip on her hand tightening. "He could've killed you. You understand that?"

"Yeah. I think I got that part." She huffed. "And it's your fault, right?"

He didn't speak, but a muscle spasmed in his jaw.

She sat up in the bed, refusing to wince at the pain in her shoulder. "And you called *me* nonsensical? Jason Nunez was in trouble, Michael. He was desperate. To his mind, it was us or him."

His eyes widened. "You're justifying his behavior?"

"Of course not. All I'm saying is that you couldn't have anticipated it. No one could have."

Michael stood there in silence for so long, Grace feared he couldn't or wouldn't listen anymore. Shoulders slumped, he raised his head. Grace held her breath at the naked pain in his eyes.

"I don't know if I can forgive myself for what happened to you," he whispered, his voice thick.

She tugged on his arm and brought his fingers to her lips, her eyes boring into his. "Listen to me, Michael. Wherever they think they're going to send me? I'm. Not. Going. Without. You," she said fiercely. "And when this is all over, we move forward. Build our home. Our future. Together."

Michael shook his head then traced her bruises gently with his finger, his eyes filled with doubt and pain. And a glimmer of hope. Grace didn't move. Barely breathed.

"Are you always going to be this bossy?" His voice hitched, but one corner of his mouth twitched up, and Grace knew she'd won. *They'd won.*

She pulled him toward her and kissed him with all the love in her heart. "I think, Detective Venetti, you're going to have to stick around to find out."

THE END

About the Author

Michelle Grey is an avid lover of books, and had always thought that someday she would take up her pen and write romantic suspense. In 2009, Michelle was diagnosed with a rare form of ovarian cancer, and she realized that "somedays" aren't guaranteed. This life changing event motivated Michelle to pursue her dream of becoming an author. Now a cancer survivor, Michelle uses her author platform to promote awareness of ovarian cancer and its symptoms.

Michelle lives in the Midwestern United States with her husband of thirty years, and has four amazing and unique children, a wonderful son-in-law, and two beautiful granddaughters. Michelle believes that any day that involves family, writing, or reading is a great day, indeed.

Want to learn more? Follow Michelle on her website or social media:
www.authormichellegrey.com
www.facebook.com/michellegreyauthor
https://twitter.com/MichelleGrey13
https://www.instagram.com/authormichellegrey/
Or sign up to stay current with her quarterly newsletter: http://bit.ly/michellegreynewslettersignup

Other Titles by Michelle Grey
Dangerous Ally (Long Shot Series, Book 1)
Unspoken Bonds (Long Shot Series, Book 2)
Convergence (Long Shot Series, Book 3)

Made in the USA
Columbia, SC
13 August 2018